Allison Leslie was her real name,
but nearly everyone called her Shorty.
She *was* short. Very, *very* short.
She was by far the shortest person in
Room 6, and she was beginning to feel
quite upset about it.

"I'm just so sick of being short,"
she thought. "I can't see things. I can't
reach things. I can't find people in a
crowd. Everyone calls me Shorty, and
people keep telling me how to grow.
But nothing works. I'm just going to be
short for ever and ever."

"How come I'm so short?" she grumbled to her mother. But her mother said, "Don't worry about it. Like mother, like daughter. We're both shorties." Then she gave Allison a hug.

3

Grandma thought that if Allison ate heaps and heaps of vegetables, she might grow taller. Allison ate vegetables until she thought they would grow out of her ears, but it didn't make any difference.

"Try to stretch yourself," said her friend Susan, who took ballet lessons. "Like this: raise both arms, point your fingers to the sky, stretch your neck and hold your head up high. Make your body tight and stand right on the tips of your toes."

Allison started walking on tiptoe wherever she went. She tiptoed and she stretched until her arms and her back ached. But still she didn't grow.

4

Allison was very unhappy. After one particularly bad day, when she'd missed out on being chosen for the class basketball team, she ran to the garden shed, flopped down behind it, and burst into tears. She didn't hear Dad coming down to the shed.

"Allison Leslie, whatever is the matter? Have you hurt yourself?" asked Dad, lifting her gently. "No!" said Allison, crying even louder. "Put me down. I'm eight, and I don't like to be carried."

"All right," said Dad, "but stop crying and tell me what's wrong. Here, use my handkerchief. Now, what's up?"

Dad listened to Allison. "Well, it *is* a bit of a problem," he said, "but remember, often the best things in life are the smallest things. Like diamonds, pearls, watches, forget-me-nots . . ."

Allison sniffed. "You're only trying to make me feel better," she said.

Then Dad had a thought. He smiled and said, "Look, Allison, I've got an idea that might take your mind off being short. Come on, you can help me."

In the shed, Dad found two long, smooth pieces of wood, and two small blocks of wood. He nailed the blocks a metre up from the ends of the long pieces.

"You hold on up here," Dad explained. "The small blocks are for your feet to stand on. Do you know what they are?"

"No," said Allison.

"They're stilts," said Dad. "When I was young, I used to have a lot of fun walking on them. Come on, I'll show you."

11

After a bit of wobbling and a bit of practice, Dad started to show off. He hopped and ran and even tried to dance.

Allison watched, fascinated.

"Now it's your turn," he said.

"All right," said Allison, while the butterflies started to flutter in her stomach.

13

Dad held the stilts while Allison put her feet on the little blocks of wood. She held on very tightly with her hands at the top of the wooden poles. It was not as easy as it looked.

"It feels really high up here. Let go, and see if I can walk."

No sooner had Dad let the stilts go than Allison toppled off.

"I didn't hurt myself," she said. "Let me try again. I'm going to keep trying until I can do it."

14

Allison tried and tried, and at last she managed to take two steps. They were wobbly steps, but she laughed with happiness.

Before long, Allison could walk the length of the driveway. At the end of the week, she went for a walk down to the bus stop.

"Good morning," she called over the fence to Mrs Harris, who was hanging out the washing.

Mrs Harris dropped the pegs. "Good gracious! Is that you, Allison? You must have grown overnight."

"Hello," she called to Mrs Thompson, who was watering the flowers with the hose.

Mrs Thompson was so
surprised, she turned to stare
and sprayed the hose over
Mr Thompson, who was dozing
in his chair on the sun-deck.

Allison's friend Susan lived next door to Mrs Thompson. Allison sneaked along the hedge on her stilts, bending as low as she could so that Susan couldn't see her coming. Then she stood up tall and looked over the bushes.

Susan was skipping and counting in a very puffed-out voice, "Ninety-five, ninety-six . . ."

"Ninety-seven, ninety-eight," said Susan and Allison together.

Susan tripped. "Allison! How did you grow that tall so quickly?"

Susan rushed over to Allison.
"What are those things?" she demanded,
with her hands on her hips.

"They're stilts. Dad made them for me."

"They're so high! Can I have a turn?"

"Sure," said Allison, "but it's pretty hard."

Susan tried, but she couldn't manage
the stilts at all.

"You just have to keep on trying,"
said Allison.

"You can try again tomorrow,
but I have to go now. I have
to practise my clown act
for the class talent show."

Away she strode on her stilts.

The night of the show arrived, and all the performers were a bit nervous. Jimmy Brown announced the acts. Soon it was Allison's turn.

Jimmy marched out on the stage and held up his hand for silence. In a big, booming voice he announced, "Ladies and gentlemen, boys and girls, we proudly present to you — Shorty the Clown!"

Susan and her friend Anna pulled back the curtains. There in the middle of the stage was a smiling Shorty the Clown, who looked very *tall* as she did tricks on stilts.

23

Everyone laughed and cheered and clapped. "More!" they all shouted.

After the show, Shorty gave Dad a hug. "Thanks, Dad" she said. "It's fun to be short *and* tall!"